Cat Tales

Smoke Cat

LINDA NEWBERY

Illustrated by Stephen Lambert

USBORNE

For Kate, Jonathan and Alexander

This edition first published in the UK in 2009 by Usborne Publishing Ltd.,
Usborne House, 83-85 Saffron Hill, London EC1N 8RT, England.
www.usborne.com

A CIP catalogue record for this book is available from the British Library.

JFMAMJJASON /08   ISBN 9780746097298   Printed in Great Britain.

Chapter One

As soon as they saw 16 Parkside Terrace, Simon's mum and dad decided that this was the house for them.

"I've always wanted to live in an old house," Dad said. "A house other people have lived in. It's like an old pair of shoes, creaky and comfortable."

Simon wasn't sure. He thought of the new houses they'd looked at, with bright clean paintwork and big windows. He'd have liked to live in one of those. But Mum said, "They've got no personality." She and Dad had the same ideas about houses, which was just as well. And this one was quite close to the flat they lived in now, so Simon wouldn't have to change schools.

Dad said, "It'll be a home, not just a house."

So they moved into the tall thin house that was more than a hundred years old. It was made of red brick and it was sandwiched between others in a row, like soldiers standing to attention. It had long narrow rooms with high ceilings, and a long narrow garden stretched behind it.

Simon's bedroom was at the back. He liked the high ceiling and the old-fashioned fireplace, but he wasn't sure about all the other people who had lived there, who'd slept in this room during its long life.

He wondered who they were, and what memories and dreams they might have left behind.

It was the fireplaces that really made up Mum's and Dad's minds. There were three – one in the main room downstairs, and one in each bedroom. Mum had always wanted a house with a real fireplace.

Standing in the downstairs room, she said, "We can have a log fire sometimes. Won't that be lovely on a cold day?"

Simon thought it would, especially when Dad talked about roasting chestnuts in the ashes. But winter was a long way off. It was early summer now, and the best thing about the house was the garden. It was much better than the bare fenced squares that went with the brand new houses, or the patch they'd shared behind the block of flats. It was a real jungle of a garden, with tangly bits and hidden corners and shadowy secret places, and a high fence separating it from next door.

Everything in the garden seemed

eager to grow as big and as high and as lush as possible. The plants in the borders spilled over on to the grass as if they'd lost their balance. Ivy and honeysuckle clambered up the fence. Flowers whose names Simon didn't know stretched up their heads to get as near to the sun as they could.

It was a garden for exploring, for crawling into the damp earthy shadowy

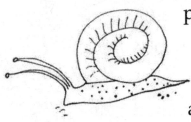

places. There were snails and slugs and spiders and worms and ladybirds and caterpillars, and once Simon found a puff of scattered feathers and a few small bones. There were

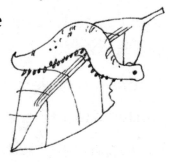

thistles and nettles and brambles and plants with thick juicy stems.

"I'll have to do something with that garden," Mum said.

Simon wondered what she meant. The garden didn't need anything done to it. Everything in the garden *knew* what to do. The plants grew, and the insects hatched and crawled and flew and nibbled.

Best of all, there was an apple tree. The blossom had finished and you could already see the new little apples coming. There were helpful branches stretching out in just the right places, so Simon could quite easily climb up to more than twice his own height above the ground, and wedge himself into a fork where the branches divided. From there, he could look down into the garden next door.

Chapter Two

Next door's garden was just as long and narrow, but not jungly. Flowers and bushes were planted all the way along its edges and in a big flower bed that was right in the middle of the lawn, like an island. Someone looked after the garden very well, Simon could tell.

An old lady was walking very slowly along the border, talking to herself. At least, that's what Simon thought she was doing. He clung tightly to the apple branch and listened.

"And how are you today, William?" the old lady asked, stopping at a rose bush with peach-coloured buds. "My goodness, you are looking glossy. The sunshine always did bring you out."

Simon looked around to see who she was talking to, but no one was there. Then she moved on, and he realized that she was talking to the *plants*.

"Charlotte, my dear," she told a long spindly straggler, "you must stand up for yourself more – this forsythia will take up all the space if you let her.

Gloria, how lovely to see you growing
so tall and strong – you're going to be a
fine lady this year. Frederick, you have a
good rest now till next spring; you've
earned it. Now, where's Blue…?"

She was quite close to Simon. She wore a long brown cardigan and a tweedy skirt, and her grey hair was so thin that the pink of her scalp gleamed through it. She stretched out her hand to touch the leaves and petals of each plant as she spoke to it. Simon saw the papery skin of her hand, and the fingers, knobbly like twigs, and the big loose ring she wore on her left hand.

Simon had heard of people talking to plants – Mum did it sometimes, to encourage the parsley she grew on the kitchen window sill. But this old lady gave them *names*. People's names. He was just wondering whether *every* plant here had a name, when the old lady turned round and saw him.

She froze, with one hand reaching towards a tall white daisy in the island bed, and stared at him.

Without meaning to let go of the
branch he was clutching, Simon found
himself slithering down from his perch
and – *Ow!* – landing on the ground with
a twist and wrench to his right ankle.

He'd grazed his hands and his knee on the apple-tree bark, and landed hard on one elbow. Flexing his ankle, he waited for a few moments, expecting the old lady's face to appear over the fence – she'd probably be cross with him for spying on her. Although he hadn't really *been* spying. All he'd been doing was climbing a tree in his own garden.

"I don't like that lady next door," he told Mum when he limped indoors.

"She talks to herself."

Mum looked surprised. "Hazel? Oh, but she's really nice. We all talk to ourselves sometimes."

Simon wasn't sure about the old lady. The name Hazel didn't suit her – she ought to be called Mrs. or Miss something. And she looked as if she'd be strict.

Chapter Three

There was an alleyway at the end of the garden, which was the way Simon came in when he got home from school.

On Thursday afternoon he let himself in at the back door to hear voices talking in the front room – Mum's and somebody else's. He went in, hoping there'd be something to eat, and saw a lady, older than Mum but not *that* old, with curly hair and bright red earrings. She was holding a mug of tea and she smelled of perfume. She smiled at him and said, "Hi, Simon," as if she'd known him for ages. "I'm Hazel from next door."

That explained it! Mum had got this lady mixed up with the other one. He'd known the old lady couldn't be called Hazel, and he couldn't imagine this one wandering round the garden talking to plants. She looked too energetic, as if she might jump up from her seat at any minute and suggest a walk to the park or a game of cricket. The other lady had seemed worn and sad.

"Hello," he said politely, really more interested in the cake on the table. It was a chocolate one with flake decoration, his favourite. "Does someone else live in your house?" he asked, when Mum

had cut him a slice.

"Just Bill," said Hazel. "My husband. Have you seen him? You can't miss him – he's a great big bloke. Rugby-playing type."

And then it occurred to Simon that perhaps she lived in the house on the *other* side – they had two next-door neighbours, after all. Perhaps he'd been the one who made the mistake, not Mum. But when Hazel left (after having a second piece of cake), Simon watched from the window, and saw her turn right and go up the path next door – the path to the house where the old lady lived.

"*She's* not the person I meant," he told Mum. "The one who was talking to herself."

Mum shrugged. "Perhaps Hazel had someone to stay."

Simon didn't think the old lady was just staying – she'd looked as if she lived there, knowing all the plants the way she did. But he  didn't think about it any more that day, because he had a new computer game, and a drawing to do for school.

He didn't think about it any more at all, until a few nights later when he woke up suddenly in the middle of the night to hear a voice calling, outside in the garden.

The old lady's voice.

He couldn't hear *what* she was calling, but it went on and on, as if to someone who didn't come.

He tried to go back to sleep, but the more he tried, the wider-awake he became. Eventually he got out of bed and pushed back the curtains.

It wasn't the middle of the night, as he'd thought. It was already starting to get light; he could make out the dim shapes of trees, fences and flower beds. And in the garden next door, the old lady, stretching out her arms and calling.

"Charlotte!" He could hear now what she was saying. "Gloria, there's a good girl. Charlotte, time to rest now. William! Here's your place. Blue! Oh, Blue, won't you come!"

She was calling to the *plants* – Simon recognized the names. It was strange enough to be standing out in the garden so early in the morning, but odder still to be calling out to *plants*. And even odder than that, if she didn't actually *live* here.

She kept bending down to touch
something. As Simon's eyes adjusted to
the first grey light he could see shapes
moving around at her feet, rubbing
against her legs – soft, fluid, furry
shadows, like cats. Although they were
shadowy, Simon could make out the
different colours: black cats, white cats,
tabby cats, pied cats, marmalade cats.
The old lady welcomed each one,
stroking it, talking to it in a soft voice,
until she was surrounded by a moving
carpet of cats, weaving, twining, purring,
arching their backs to be stroked. And
every few moments she broke off to
stand upright and gaze around,
and she called, "Blue! Blue,
won't you come?"

Simon didn't actually see them do it –
one minute they were there and the next
they were gone – but the shadowy cats
seemed to melt away into the ground, or
fade like mist, into the flower beds and
shrubbery. The old lady stood alone,
holding out her hands and looking up at
the fence between the two gardens.
"Blue! Blue, please come!"

Simon looked where she was looking,
towards the fence. Just for a
moment he
saw, balancing
there but
walking away,
a large, smoke-
grey, plume-
tailed cat, faint

as a shadow in the last few moments before the sun goes in.

"Blue!" The old lady's voice sounded despairing now. The cat disappeared into the hollies at the end of the garden, and the old lady turned towards the house. Simon couldn't see her any more.

By the time he woke up later in the morning he thought he'd dreamed the whole thing.

But, next night, the smoke cat came back by itself.

Simon had got out of bed for the toilet, and on the way back he glanced out of the window, just in case.

The moon was so bright that it threw a silvery light over the grass and the bushes. There was no old lady, no voice calling, but on the fence Simon could see the smoke cat, treading softly towards the house, balancing on delicate paws.

The cat paused, stared down into next-door's garden, rubbed itself against a fence post, then turned and walked off slowly, stopping to look back. It seemed disappointed.

"Blue! Come back!" Simon had opened the window and was shouting out before he knew why. The cat stopped, and gazed up at him for a moment, wafting its plume of a tail.

Then it walked off, along the fence, towards the hollies, where it faded and vanished like smoke melting into the air.

Watching the place where it had gone, Simon felt an ache of loneliness, although he didn't know why. There was nothing to show that Blue had ever been.

Chapter Four

Mum had a dentist's appointment, and she told Simon that she wouldn't be in when he got back from school that day. "Hazel says you can go round to her house till I get home," she told him, "and she'll get you some tea."

It was hot and sunny, and Hazel was weeding the back garden when he arrived. She stopped to fetch juice and doughnuts from the kitchen and they both went outside.

The garden looked a bit messier than Simon remembered it, although there was a bucket and a big pile of pulled weeds where Hazel had been working. He looked round, thinking that he knew some of these plants by name: Charlotte, Frederick, Gloria, William. But it would sound silly to say so. He wondered whether Hazel knew their names too.

"Did you plant all these?" he asked her.

"Goodness, no!" Hazel snipped a dead flower from one of William's branches. "It takes a long time to get a

garden looking like this. I just tidy it up now and then. No, my mother did most of the planting."

But then why hadn't she *said* that her mother lived here? He'd asked, just the other day. Perhaps the mother was upstairs having a lie-down.

"Where is she?" he asked.

Hazel looked surprised. "My mum? Oh, she's not here now. She used to live with us, but she died two years ago."

Simon nearly said, "But she can't have done. I've seen her," until he realized

that this was impossible; and besides,
Hazel must know. He couldn't think
what to say. He looked towards the
house as if the old lady might come out
of the shadows. But no one was there.

"Does – I mean did – your mother like cats?" he asked.

Hazel gave him a look of astonishment. "Yes! She was dotty about them. How did you guess?"

"Er – I just wondered." Simon was beginning to feel a bit peculiar.

"Yes, she had dozens of cats over the years," Hazel said, looking towards Charlotte. "Four or five at a time. Of course they died sometimes, usually of old age. Whenever that happened she'd go to the garden centre and buy a new shrub and plant it, in memory – so nearly every plant in the garden's got a cat attached to it, if you see what I mean." Hazel gave a little laugh, as if she thought Simon might find this silly.

"She even called the plants by the cats' names. Gloria, I remember…Frederick… I can't remember half of them now."

Simon wondered what she would say if he added, "Well, there's Charlotte, and there's William…" But he didn't say anything. He was wondering about Blue. Why wouldn't Blue come into the garden like the others? What did Blue *want*?

"She had a lovely cat just before she died," Hazel said. "A long-haired fluffy cat – grey, or more like blue-grey. She called him Blue."

"Yes, I know. I've seen him." This time the words were out of Simon's mouth before he could stop them.

Hazel stared at him.

"No, you can't have done," she said. "Blue died, a few weeks after Mum did. He wasn't very old. I don't know if a cat can pine, but I'm sure Blue pined for her." She frowned. "Maybe there's another cat around that looks like him. But he was an unusual cat, not the sort you see very often."

No, it was definitely Blue. Simon didn't say it, but he thought it. And then, like a whisper, he saw the smoke cat, a shadowy, furry shape creeping out from

the deep shade of the hollies and wafting
along the fence like a curl of smoke.

"There he is!" Simon shouted, before
he could stop himself.

Hazel whipped round and looked
straight at Blue, who paused, one paw
lifted, and stared back. Then Hazel
turned to Simon, half-smiling,
half-puzzled.

"There's nothing there. You're having a game with me."

"I'm not. He *is* there! Look!"

Just as before, Blue tightrope-walked along the fence, hesitated as if about to jump down into the garden, then stopped. His mouth opened in a silent

 miaow and he turned himself around on the spot and walked away. Just as before, Simon had the sense that Blue was disappointed. With a lash of his plume tail, Blue stepped carefully along the fence towards the deep shade of the

hollies. Simon's eyes followed the blurry shape until he couldn't be sure it had ever been there.

Hazel had got tired of the joke she thought he was playing, and had gone back to her weeding, not noticing.

Just then Mum arrived from the dentist's, with her mouth all lopsided from the injection she'd had. "Come on, Shimon," she said, keeping her mouth shut as tight as a ventriloquist's. "It'sh time to go home. Thanksh for having him, Hashel."

Indoors, Simon ran up to his room
and looked out of the window, thinking
about what Hazel had told him. It was
obvious that she hadn't seen or heard
the old lady; nor did she see the smoke

cat on the fence. As far as he could tell, he was the only person who saw them. It gave him the odd feeling that he was supposed to find an answer. Blue wanted something, and Simon knew that he was the only person who could guess what it was.

Chapter Five

In the days and nights that followed, the old lady and the cat came back several times. There was no pattern to it. Sometimes, when Simon heard the old lady calling, it was in the middle of the night. Sometimes it was in broad sunlight, and she'd be there in the garden for anyone to see, if only anyone else *could* see. Once, when Simon was watching from the apple tree, Hazel's husband Bill brushed past her without noticing.

Sometimes the old lady was on her own, talking to the plants; sometimes she was surrounded by her purring carpet of cats. But always she called for Blue, and always Blue turned away, disappointed. The old lady and Blue became so much a part of Simon's thoughts that he didn't know whether he dreamed them or really saw them. He only knew that he had to help in some way – that he was the only person who *could*.

One afternoon, in desperation, he

chased Blue right down the garden. It was useless; he should have known. Blue vanished like a wisp of smoke into the evergreen depths of the hollies, and Simon plunged through the bushes on his own side of the fence, shouting, "Blue! Blue! Wait!" Even while he was shouting he knew that the smoke cat wouldn't wait; and he didn't know what he'd have done if somehow he'd caught Blue. You can't catch and keep a ghost cat; and you can't make it stay.

At the end of the chase Simon was deep in the thickest and thorniest bushes, with his face scratched, his T-shirt snagged and his knees and hands grazed and stung.

Blue was nowhere to be seen.

Mum stared at him when he went indoors. "What on earth have you been doing?" She didn't sound too pleased. "You look as if you've been dragged through a hedge backwards."

Well, yes – forwards, anyway.

But it was too hard to explain; who'd

believe him? "Just playing in the garden," was all he said.

"Well, I wish you'd put something old on first," Mum said, still a bit cross. "That T-shirt used to be quite smart." She was collecting her things together: purse, bag, keys. "D'you want to come and help me choose a present for Hazel? It's her birthday on Sunday and she's invited us round."

"Where'll you look for it?" Simon asked suspiciously. He didn't fancy trailing round shops.

"I thought I'd go to the garden centre," Mum said. "Hazel's so keen on gardening – always out there digging and planting."

Simon wasn't sure why he agreed to

go – garden centres weren't the most exciting places – but nevertheless he did. This one was huge, with garden chairs and tools inside, and long avenues outside stretching into the distance, labelled *Climbers* or *Herbaceous Perennials*.

Mum started looking at hanging baskets bursting with geraniums and petunias, but Simon's attention was caught by the bigger plants, all lined up in rows and labelled with their names. He found himself thinking, *There's a Charlotte*, and, *That rose over there's a bit like William*.

Then it occurred to him.

Blue didn't *have* a plant like the other cats, because the old lady had died first

and hadn't been able to get him one. All
the other cats came home to their own
plant, but Blue always went away
disappointed.

Here's my chance! Simon thought. *I'll have to make Mum buy a Blue plant.*

He walked along the rows, looking for a plant to suit the smoke cat. There was row after row of yellow-flowered shrubs, pink-flowered climbers, scarlet perennials, some plants with no flowers at all. Nothing that would do. His spirits sank. If he didn't find the right plant here, where could he find it?

And then, turning a corner, he saw it at the end of a row ahead of him.

It was so obviously the right plant for Blue that it seemed to call out to him. It had clusters of flowers like puffs of blue smoke, floating in a haze against darker leaves. He bent down as if greeting it, stroked the leaves, then turned over the label and read it.

Ceanothus Blue Smoke.

Just right.

A smoke plant for the smoke cat.

He tracked down Mum, who was looking at some garish marigolds, and said, "I've found it! Just what Hazel wants."

"I was thinking perhaps a nice planted arrangement…"

"No. This is what she wants!"

Simon dragged her by the hand to where the special plant was waiting. Mum was still looking back longingly  at the brassy marigolds, but in the end she gave in and got out her purse, and Simon carried *Ceanothus Blue Smoke* to the counter inside.

Chapter Six

Next day, at Hazel's, Simon couldn't wait for *Ceanothus Blue Smoke* to be planted. The garden table was loaded with all sorts of delicious things, and Hazel's husband Bill had bought a special cake with candles on it. Usually Simon's stomach would have started

gurgling with delight, but not today
– not yet. Blue's plant must come first.

"But I haven't decided where to put it
yet," Hazel said, laughing.

"I'll help you," Simon said. He
dragged her towards the island bed and
pointed. "Look, there. Just between
Charlotte and Gloria. Blue's going to get
quite big, so he'll need a bit of space."

Hazel stared at him. "Blue?"

"Yes. *You know.*" He looked at Hazel hard, meaning *Don't say anything to Mum and Dad – they won't understand.*

She looked at him oddly, then nodded and went and fetched a spade and a bag of bedding compost. Simon helped with the digging – the ground was hard and dry – and when the hole was big enough, Hazel's expert fingers arranged the earth around

Ceanothus Blue Smoke's roots as if she were tucking it into bed.

Soon the new plant was firmly in its place, looking quite at home – cosily nestling between its two larger neighbours, but with plenty of room to grow.

"Is it teatime yet?" Simon's dad said, looking hungrily at the iced cake. "I had no idea you were so keen on gardening, Simon. There's plenty for you to do to our own jungle, if you want to get cracking. There's weeding and mowing and pruning and—"

"No, thanks," Simon said hastily. "I only like this one plant."

He'd done the best he could, but now he wanted to see if it worked. When Hazel had blown out her candles and the cake had been cut and most of it eaten,

Simon and his parents went home. A little later, when the daylight started to fade, Simon went up to his room and looked out.

Nothing was happening. The garden table was still there, the chairs around it; Hazel's spade and compost-bag were beside the island bed where she had left them. There was no old lady, no smoke cat.

"Oh, come on, Blue!" Simon whispered, his mouth against the window. "I haven't gone to all this trouble for *nothing* – you *must* come…"

Obstinately, the shadows refused to quiver into life and gather themselves into the shape of a smoke cat. There was just a bare fence, and the hollies.

Then he heard, very faintly, "Charlotte, come along! William, there's a good boy! Gloria, where've you been?"

He craned his neck as far as he could.
There she was, Hazel's mother, in her
baggy cardigan and her droopy skirt,
walking out from the patio into the
dusk. The dim light streamed with
shapes, surging, leaping down to the
grass, twining, tails high. The old lady
walked as far as the island bed, and
then she saw
Ceanothus Blue Smoke.
She paused, and
stretched out
a hand to
touch it
as if she
wasn't sure
it was real.

Simon hardly dared breathe.

The shadows by the hollies quivered and shook themselves into the shadowy shape of a cat.

Blue.

He sat, paused, then trotted along the fence with his plume tail held high.

"Blue! Blue, come down!" The old lady's voice was hopeful, not despairing.

Blue hesitated, opened his mouth in a silent miaow, and bounded down into the garden, where his shadowy shape merged with the other cats. Hazel's mother bent down to stroke him, and the smoke cat took one joyful leap and landed lightly on her shoulders, twining himself around her ears.

Just for a second, Simon thought the old lady looked up towards his window, and he saw her fleeting smile. He waved back. The whole garden was filled with purring.

Then Simon blinked, and nothing was there at all; just the silent gardens, and the dim shape of the smoke bush, and a rising moon.

About the author

Linda Newbery loves to write. She also loves her four cats: Holly, Hazel, Finn and Fleur who keep her busy and who have inspired Cat Tales. Linda had her first novel published in 1988 and she's the author of many books for young readers. She has won the Silver Medal Nestlé Children's Book Prize and the Costa Children's Book Award.

Linda writes in a hut in her garden, usually with a cat or two for company.

Cat Tales

Curl up with Cat Tales from award-winning and enchanting storyteller, Linda Newbery.

The Cat with Two Names

Two of everything sounds perfect, but it soon leads to double the trouble for Cat...

ISBN 9780746096147

Rain Cat

Nobody believes that the mysterious cat can control the weather...until it starts to rain!

ISBN 9780746097281

Smoke Cat

Where do the shadowy cats in next door's garden come from and why won't one particular cat join them?

ISBN 9780746097298

Shop Cat

Strange things have started happening in the toy shop since Twister came to stay...

ISBN 9780746097304

And coming soon...

The Cat who Wasn't There

Vincent is so lonely without his cat, Snow... until a slim white cat appears in his garden.

ISBN 9780746097328

Ice Cat

Tom's cat is made of snow and ice, so of course it can't come alive...or can it?

ISBN 9780746097311

All priced at £3.99

For more fun and furry
animal stories, log on to
www.fiction.usborne.com